THE GRAPHIC
SHAKESPEARE SERIES

MUCH ADO
ABOUT NOTHING

Published by
Evans Brothers Limited
2A Portman Mansions
Chiltern Street
London W1U 6NR

Reprinted 2007

Designed by Brian Shields.

British Library Cataloguing in Publication Data
Burningham, Hilary
  Much Ado About Nothing. – (The Graphic Shakespeare series)
  1. Shakespeare, William, 1564-1616. Much Ado About Nothing - Juvenile literature
  2. Courtship - Italy - Messina - Juvenile literature
  3. Children's stories
  I. Title
  823.9'14 [J]

  ISBN 978 0 237 53043 3

Printed in China by WKT Company Limited.

THE GRAPHIC
SHAKESPEARE SERIES

MUCH ADO
ABOUT NOTHING

RETOLD BY HILARY BURNINGHAM
ILLUSTRATED BY TRACY FENNELL

Evans

EVANS BROTHERS LIMITED

THE CHARACTERS IN THE PLAY

Leonato's Household

Signor Leonato	– Governor of Messina
Signor Antonio	– his brother
Hero	– Leonato's only daughter
Beatrice	– an orphan, Leonato's niece
Margaret	
Ursula	} – Hero's attendants
Friar Francis (The Friar)	– a priest

The Military

Don Pedro	– Prince of Arragon
Don John	– his bastard* brother
Count Claudio of Florence	
Count Benedick of Padua	} – young lords, companions of Don Pedro
Borachio	
Conrade	} – followers of Don John
Messenger	
Balthasar	– a singer

The Town

Dogberry	– Constable of Messina
Verges	– Deputy Constable
The Sexton	– Town Clerk
The Watch	– the night watchmen on duty

* In Shakespeare's time, a person whose parents were not married to each other was called a bastard.

PORTRAIT GALLERY

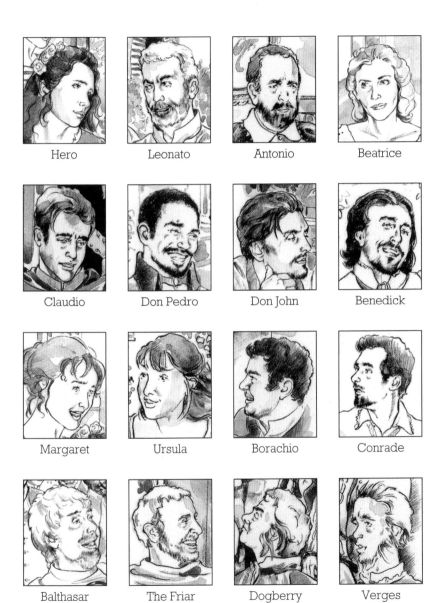

Hero

Leonato

Antonio

Beatrice

Claudio

Don Pedro

Don John

Benedick

Margaret

Ursula

Borachio

Conrade

Balthasar

The Friar

Dogberry

Verges

ACT 1

There was great excitement in the small Italian town of Messina. Don Pedro, Prince of Arragon, was to visit the town on his way home from war.

Leonato, the governor of the town, questioned the Prince's messenger. He learned that the Prince had defeated his enemies, with very few casualties among his officers and men. A young man named Claudio had surprised everyone with his bravery.

Leonato's niece, Beatrice, enquired about Benedick, one of Don Pedro's officers. She had a very sharp tongue[1] and made fun of Benedick, whom she clearly disliked. Leonato told the messenger that this was a playful game between Beatrice and Benedick, a kind of war of words. The messenger remarked that he would rather be Beatrice's friend than her enemy.

There was no time to prepare. The Prince had arrived.

[1]a sharp tongue – she could be very sarcastic

LEONATO: You must not, sir, mistake my niece. There is a kind of merry war betwixt Signor Benedick and her; they never meet but there's a skirmish of wit between them.

Don Pedro and his followers were warmly greeted by Leonato and his household.

Immediately, Beatrice and Benedick began to quarrel, each trying to outdo the other with a witty remark. Don Pedro interrupted their argument to announce that Leonato had invited them all to be his guests. He and his friends would stay for at least a month.

Leonato especially welcomed Don John, who was the Prince's half-brother[1]. He and the Prince had recently made friends after being enemies for some time.

Leonato led the guests into his home.

[1]half-brother – they had the same father, but different mothers

BEATRICE: ...I had rather hear my dog bark at a crow than a man swear he loves me.

BENEDICK: God keep your ladyship still in that mind! So some gentleman or other shall 'scape a predestinate scratched face.

Claudio could not take his eyes off Hero, Leonato's daughter. She was both beautiful and charming. Already, he thought himself in love with her, and asked Benedick to help him get her for his wife. Benedick tried to change Claudio's mind. He hated the idea of marriage, and anyway thought Beatrice more beautiful than Hero[1]. Don Pedro, on the other hand, thought Hero would be a very suitable wife for Claudio. As Leonato's only child, she would inherit all his lands and money.

Don Pedro suggested that he could help Claudio instead. Leonato was making great preparations for a party that night. Everyone would be wearing masks. Don Pedro, pretending to be Claudio, would speak to Hero in order to find out her feelings. If she said that she loved Claudio, he, Don Pedro, would then ask Leonato for her hand in marriage. In this way, he was sure that Hero would be promised to Claudio.

[1]This is our first indication that, in spite of their arguing, Benedick finds Beatrice attractive.

DON PEDRO: If thou dost love fair Hero, cherish it,
And I will break with her and with her father
And thou shalt have her.

Leonato's brother, Antonio, brought him important news. One of Antonio's servants had overheard a conversation between Don Pedro and Count Claudio. According to the servant, Don Pedro was in love with Hero[1]. That very night at the party, he planned to ask her to marry him.

Leonato was excited to think that the Prince wanted to marry his daughter. He must prepare her. He was sure she would like to marry the Prince.

A group of musicians led by Balthasar the singer passed by. They were to entertain the guests and play the music for dancing at Leonato's big party.

[1]The audience knows that Antonio's servant has mistaken the meaning of the overheard conversation. Don Pedro planned to speak to Hero in order to 'get' her for Claudio.

ANTONIO: ...the Prince discovered to Claudio that he loved my niece, your daughter, and meant to acknowledge it this night in a dance...

Conrade, Don John's follower, wondered why his master seemed miserable. Don John said that he could see no reason to be happy, therefore he would be sad. He behaved exactly as he felt without worrying what others thought.

Conrade pointed out that Don John's half-brother, Don Pedro, had recently become more friendly. Don John should try to keep the friendship of his powerful brother. Don John was scornful. He had no intention of changing in order to please others. He would remain as he was: villainous[1] and discontented.

Borachio, Don John's other follower, rushed in. He had just overheard Don Pedro tell Claudio that he would speak to Hero, find out her feelings, and 'win' her for Claudio.

Don John was angry. Claudio was becoming more important than he himself. Perhaps with this news, he could find a way to make trouble for Claudio.

[1]villainous – evil

DON JOHN: That young upstart hath all the glory of my overthrow; if I can cross him any way, I bless myself every way.

ACT 2

After the excellent banquet, Leonato was chatting to his brother Antonio, Hero, Beatrice and their friends. The women commented that Don John was melancholy[1] and quiet. Beatrice said that a man half way between Don John, who was too quiet, and Benedick, who talked too much, would be very attractive, especially if he had good legs and lots of money!

Beatrice was firmly of the opinion that, as she had no respect for men anyway, she was happier unmarried.

Antonio was sure that his niece, Hero, was different. She would obey her father in these matters. Only, said Beatrice, so long as Leonato chose the right man for her, otherwise Hero should please herself.

Leonato reminded Hero that the Prince was planning to ask her to marry him. As her father, he told her he would like her to say yes.

The dance was about to start. They all put on their masks.

[1]melancholy – sad, gloomy

BEATRICE: Yes, faith; it is my cousin's duty to make curtsy and say, 'Father, as it please you.' But yet for all that, cousin, let him be a handsome fellow, or else make another curtsy and say, 'Father, as it please me'.

When the dancing began, Don Pedro took Hero aside as he had planned.

Nearby, Don John recognised Claudio underneath his mask, but pretended to mistake him for Benedick. He told 'Benedick' (really Claudio) that Don Pedro had fallen in love with Hero. Hero was of a lower social rank than the Prince, therefore 'Benedick' should try to persuade the Prince not to marry her. Don John was trying to make Claudio suspicious of the Prince.

Left alone, Claudio removed his mask. He believed Don John. The Prince had fallen in love with Hero and wanted to win her for himself. He would have her; Claudio would not. Claudio felt angry and miserable.

Then Benedick came to join Claudio and told him the same thing: Don Pedro and Hero were in love.

Deeply upset, Claudio walked away to be alone.

CLAUDIO: Thus answer I in name of Benedick,
But hear these ill news with the ears of Claudio.
'Tis certain so; the Prince woos for himself.

Almost immediately, Don Pedro, Leonato and Hero came looking for Benedick. Beatrice had been making trouble. She had told Don Pedro that the gentleman she had danced with had informed her that Benedick had been very rude about her. Don Pedro criticised Benedick, who flew into a rage. He himself had danced with Beatrice, and knew this to be completely untrue. He said that speaking with her made him feel like a man being shot with arrows.

Beatrice returned with Claudio. Sarcastically calling Beatrice 'my Lady Tongue', Benedick took himself away.

Don Pedro, teasing Beatrice, said that she appeared to have lost the love of Signor Benedick. She, looking sad, confided that once she had loved him, but he had not been true to her. She would not make the same mistake again.

DON PEDRO: Come, lady, come; you have lost the heart of
Signor Benedick.
BEATRICE: Indeed, my lord, he lent it me awhile, and I gave
him use for it, a double heart for his single one.

Don Pedro had asked Beatrice to bring Claudio to him in order to give him good news, but first he teased him a little, asking why he looked so sad. Claudio would not give an explanation.

At last, Don Pedro told him that he had spoken to Hero on Claudio's behalf, and also to Leonato, who had agreed to the marriage.

Claudio, who had lost all hope, was speechless with happiness. Hero whispered that she loved him too.

CLAUDIO: Silence is the perfectest herald of joy; I were but little happy, if I could say how much. Lady, as you are mine, I am yours; I give away myself for you and dote upon the exchange.

Seeing the happiness of Claudio and Hero, Beatrice mocked herself for still having no husband. Don Pedro had begun to admire this amusing woman who didn't seem to care what she said. He offered to marry her himself. As usual Beatrice had an answer: she would need another husband, she said, for weekdays, as the Prince was much too important to be a husband every day.

After Beatrice had left, the Prince told Leonato how pleasant she was. She would make an excellent wife for Benedick, if only they didn't annoy each other so much. Leonato joked that after a week of marriage they would drive each other mad.

Claudio wanted to marry Hero straight away, but Leonato had many preparations to make. The wedding would take place in a week's time.

The Prince had decided that Beatrice and Benedick would be a good match for each other. He had worked out a plan to make them fall in love and asked the others to help him.

DON PEDRO: She were an excellent wife for Benedick.
LEONATO: O Lord, my lord, if they were but a week
married, they would talk themselves mad.

Don John was angry that Claudio was to marry Hero. Borachio, however, thought he knew a way to disgrace Hero and so prevent the marriage. He explained his plan.

Don John was to tell the Prince and Count Claudio that Hero was a wicked woman. Of course, they would want proof. Margaret, Hero's attendant, was Borachio's girlfriend. He would persuade her to dress up as Hero and appear, kissing him, at Hero's window. Calling him Claudio, she would speak to him as if they were lovers. Don John, for his part, was to make sure that the real Claudio, and Don Pedro, saw this. They would think that Hero was unfaithful to Claudio.

The best thing, said Borachio, would be to arrange this drama the very night before the wedding. Don John was pleased with the plan and promised to pay Borachio a thousand ducats[1] for his trickery.

[1]ducats – gold coins, in use in Shakespeare's time. A thousand ducats is about £1,500.

DON JOHN: Grow this to what adverse issue it can, I will put it in practice. Be cunning in working this, and thy fee is a thousand ducats.

Benedick walked in the orchard, thinking how much Claudio had changed. Like himself, Claudio had always laughed at people who fell in love. Now, he had fallen in love with Hero. Instead of being interested in everything to do with war, such as marching, military music and suits of armour, all he thought about was fashionable clothes and dance music. From plain speaking, he now spoke like a poet or even a teacher. Benedick thought that no woman would ever bring about such a change in him.

Hearing Don Pedro and the others coming Benedick hid behind some trees, not wanting to be seen. They spotted him at once. From then on, they knew that Benedick could hear everything they said.

Balthasar came along, carrying his lute. They asked him to sing one of their favourite songs. After the song, Don Pedro told Balthasar to choose some special music for the following evening. They were going to serenade[1] Lady Hero at her bedroom window.

[1]serenade – sing under a lady's window. (This fitted in perfectly with Don John's plans.)

BALTHASAR: *The Song*
Sigh no more, ladies, sigh no more,
   Men were deceivers ever,
One foot in sea and one on shore,
   To one thing constant never:
Then sigh not so, but let them go,
   And be you blithe and bonny,
Converting all your sounds of woe
   Into Hey nonny, nonny.

After Balthasar's song, knowing Benedick could hear, Don Pedro loudly asked Leonato if his niece, Beatrice, was in love with Benedick. Leonato replied that she doted[1] on Signor Benedick, even though she pretended not to like him.

Benedick could hardly believe his ears. At first he thought it was a trick, but surely Don Pedro and Leonato were too serious and honourable to play tricks.

Then, Don Pedro and Claudio spoke about Beatrice and her 'love' for Benedick. For example, Hero had told Leonato and Claudio how Beatrice sighed and cried for Benedick and even tried to write love letters to him. Hero was afraid that Beatrice would make herself ill, she was so in love. Then they all wondered (loudly) whether Benedick was good enough for her.

Don Pedro, Claudio and Leonato went to dinner, leaving Benedick to think about what he had overheard.

[1]doted on – loved very much

CLAUDIO: (to Don Pedro and Leonato) He hath ta'en the infection; hold it up.

DON PEDRO: Hath she made her affection known to Benedick?

LEONATO: No, and swears she never will; that's her torment.

Benedick was completely taken in by Don Pedro's little trick. He started to believe that Beatrice was in love with him as they had said. More to the point, he realised that they were right – Beatrice was a fine woman. Perhaps he could even change his mind about marriage. It would be very easy to fall in love with Beatrice.

The lady herself appeared. Don Pedro had told her to tell Benedick that dinner was served. She didn't want to come, she told Benedick. Don Pedro had insisted.

She spoke to Benedick just as she usually did, but Benedick, after Don Pedro's conversation, imagined different meanings in everything she said. He became more and more sure that she loved him – and that thought made him very, very happy.

BENEDICK: Fair Beatrice, I thank you for your pains.
BEATRICE: I took no more pains for those thanks than you take pains to thank me; if it had been painful, I would not have come.

ACT 3

Hero and her ladies-in-waiting, Margaret and Ursula, also took part in Don Pedro's plan to bring Beatrice and Benedick together.

Hero and Ursula went for a walk in the orchard. Margaret persuaded Beatrice to follow and listen to their conversation. Knowing that Beatrice was nearby, Hero and Ursula began to set the trap. Hero said that Benedick's friends were very worried. He was hopelessly in love with Beatrice. Unfortunately, Beatrice found fault with every man she met. Benedick was too good, said Hero, to be hurt by Beatrice and her sharp tongue. They must find a way to make him fall out of love. Ursula agreed.

Beatrice was saddened by their conversation. Was she really as cruel as they had said? But, she thought joyfully, if Benedick loved her and she loved him in return, that would change everything.

BEATRICE: (coming forward)
        What fire is in mine ears? Can this be true?
          Stand I condemned for pride and scorn so much?
        Contempt, farewell! and maiden pride, adieu!
          No glory lives behind the back of such.
        And, Benedick, love on; I will requite thee,
          Taming my wild heart to thy loving hand.

Don Pedro announced that straight after the wedding he would leave for Arragon. Claudio offered to go with him but Don Pedro said it would not be fair to ask him to leave Hero, his bride, straight after their marriage. He would ask Benedick to accompany him instead. In fact, he was testing Benedick to see if his feelings for Beatrice were changing.

Already, Benedick seemed different. Everyone noticed that he had shaved off his beard and was wearing fashionable clothes. He was even using perfume and cosmetics.

Benedick walked away with Leonato to have a chat. Don Pedro was sure that his plan was working and that Benedick wanted to tell Leonato about his new feelings for Beatrice.

Claudio reported that Hero, Ursula, and Margaret had carried out their part of the plan with Beatrice. Perhaps when Beatrice and Benedict next met they would not immediately start to argue.

DON PEDRO: Hath any man seen him at the barber's?
CLAUDIO: No, but the barber's man hath been seen with
           him and the old ornament of his cheek hath
           already stuffed tennis balls.

Like Don Pedro, Don John had a plan, but his was a cruel one. He began by telling Claudio that Hero was unfaithful to him. He could prove it, he said, if Claudio went with him that night to Leonato's house. What he would see there would make him change his mind about marrying her.

Angrily, Claudio said that if Don John was speaking the truth, he would shame Hero at their wedding the next day. In front of all the wedding guests, he would refuse to marry her.

CLAUDIO: If I see any thing tonight why I should not marry her, tomorrow in the congregation, where I should wed, there will I shame her.

DON PEDRO: And, as I wooed for thee to obtain her, I will join with thee to disgrace her.

Later that night, a man called Dogberry was giving the night watchmen their orders. The Watch was a group of men who went round the streets at night to make sure there was no trouble. They called at the alehouses[1], sending everyone home to bed. Dogberry was a large man who thought himself very important. Verges, who was much smaller and thinner, was his faithful sidekick[2].

Dogberry told his men not to talk too much among themselves, or they would disturb people. His men replied that they would sleep instead. Dogberry said he thought that would be alright[3].

He told some of his men to guard Leonato's house. Leonato's daughter, the Lady Hero[4], would be married the next day and Dogberry didn't want any trouble. Satisfied that everything was arranged, Dogberry and Verges went on their way.

[1]alehouses – pubs
[2]sidekick – a person's assistant or junior associate (slang, U.S.A.)
[3]Shakespeare is making fun of Dogberry. A sleeping night watchman is not much good!
[4]Lady Hero – Hero was the daughter of the governor, therefore Dogberry would call her Lady Hero.

DOGBERRY: You shall also make no noise in the streets; for the watch to babble and to talk is most tolerable and not to be endured.

FIRST WATCHMAN: We will rather sleep than talk; we know what belongs to a watch,

Later, during the watch, Borachio and Conrade appeared. The watchmen were suspicious. What were these two up to? They stood back and listened.

Borachio was very pleased with himself. His plan had worked[1]. He and Margaret, Hero's lady-in-waiting, had appeared at Hero's window, kissing and cuddling. Don John had made sure that the Prince and Claudio were below and had seen them. They had thought that Margaret was Hero.

Claudio was furious. He said that he would go to church the next morning and tell all the wedding guests that Hero was wicked. He would refuse to marry her.

Borachio was pleased. He had earned his thousand ducats from Don John.

The watchmen were horrified. Borachio's actions were disgraceful. An innocent woman's life would be ruined. It would bring shame on all Leonato's family. They arrested Borachio and Conrade immediately and took them away.

[1]In Shakespeare's play, the audience doesn't actually see the plan being carried out. Instead, they hear Borachio's account of it. Some directors show the deception taking place.

BORACHIO: ...away went Claudio enraged; swore he would meet her, as he was appointed, next morning at the temple, and there, before the whole congregation, shame her with what he saw o'er night, and send her home again without a husband.

It was 5 o'clock the next morning and Hero was preparing for her wedding. Her ladies-in-waiting Margaret and Ursula were helping her.

Soon, they were joined by Beatrice, who was acting strangely. Margaret was talking a great deal. Their plot to get Beatrice and Benedick together was on her mind. Several times she almost gave the game away, by referring to marriage and talking about Benedick. Several times, Beatrice seemed to be suspicious. She was not witty as she usually was, and made the excuse that she had a bad cold.

Margaret commented that both Beatrice and Benedick seemed to have changed recently. Were they by any chance in love? Beatrice claimed she was talking in riddles and became exasperated.

Ursula announced that all the important people of the town were gathered together, waiting for Hero. It was time to go to the church.

MARGARET: ...how you may be converted I know not,
but me thinks you look with your eyes as other
women do.

BEATRICE: What pace is this that thy tongue keeps?

MARGARET: Not a false gallop.

Leonato was in a hurry. It was his daughter's wedding day. He was annoyed to be stopped by the talkative Dogberry and his sidekick, Verges.

The night before, they told him, the night watchmen had arrested two suspicious persons[1]. They wanted Leonato to question the prisoners. Leonato refused. He was too busy with his daughter's wedding[2]. Before hurrying away, he told them to question the prisoners themselves.

[1]Conrade and Borachio
[2]The audience knows that if Leonato had time to listen, he would learn about the trick played on Claudio and Don Pedro. This creates suspense.

DOGBERRY: One word, sir; our watch, sir, have indeed
comprehended two aspicious persons, and
we would have them this morning examined
before your worship.

LEONATO: Take their examination yourself and bring it
me; I am now in great haste, as it may appear
unto you.

ACT 4

All the important people of Messina were gathered at the church for Hero and Claudio's wedding.

The Friar[1] asked Claudio and Hero if either of them knew of any reason why they should not be married. Hero said that she knew of no reason. To everyone's surprise, Claudio had a shocking announcement to make. Hero had been unfaithful to him. She was a wanton[2], he declared.

Leonato tried to defend his daughter, but Claudio wouldn't listen. Hero was crying and confused. She thought Claudio must be ill.

Claudio asked Hero who she had been talking with at her window the night before. No one, insisted Hero.

Don Pedro, Don John, and Claudio all repeated the accusation until at last Leonato asked for a dagger to kill himself. He believed their story.

Hero, overcome with shame, fainted and fell to the ground as if she were dead. Don John hurried Don Pedro and Claudio away. His plan had succeeded.

[1]Friar – a clergyman, a priest
[2]wanton – a woman who would have sex with anyone

CLAUDIO: What man was he talked with you yesternight
           Out at your window betwixt twelve and one?
           Now, if you are a maid, answer to this.
HERO: I talked with no man at that hour, my lord.

In spite of everything, the Friar believed Hero to be innocent. He asked who she was accused of being unfaithful with, but she had no idea. The Friar was more and more sure that there had been a terrible mistake.

Benedick had a thought. Don Pedro and Claudio were known to be honourable men but Don John the Bastard, as they called him, was known to be a villain[1]. Perhaps Don John had somehow tricked the others[2].

The Friar had an idea. A few minutes before, Hero had fainted and many people thought she had died of shame. Leonato must carry on the pretence, mourning her, and telling everyone that her body was in the family tomb[3]. Claudio and the others would begin to remember how good and beautiful Hero was. They might even begin to feel sorry for what had happened.

Leonato was weak with grief. He agreed to the Friar's plan. The Friar spoke comforting words to Hero, trying to give her hope.

[1]villain – bad or evil person
[2]Benedick had guessed correctly!
[3]family tomb – rich families had a special small building called a tomb, where the bodies of their family were placed.

FRIAR: Pause awhile,
And let my counsel sway you in this case.
Your daughter here the Princes left for dead;
Let her awhile by secretly kept in,
And publish it that she is dead indeed.

The others left to follow the Friar's instructions. Beatrice and Benedick were alone together. Benedick wanted to do something, do anything, to make Beatrice feel better. Beatrice had no doubt what he should do. She wanted revenge. Benedick must kill Claudio.

At first, Benedick could not accept the idea. He loved Beatrice and wanted desperately to please her, but Claudio was his friend.

Beatrice was sure that Claudio's accusations were untrue. If only she were a man, so that she could get revenge herself. Benedick asked Beatrice if she truly, in her heart, believed what she was saying. When Beatrice said most strongly that indeed she did, Benedick agreed to challenge Claudio to a duel[1]. And he would spread the word that Hero was dead.

[1]duel – a fight between two people, usually to the death

BENEDICK: Enough, I am engaged; I will challenge him.
I will kiss your hand, and so I leave you. By this
hand, Claudio shall render me a dear account.
As you hear of me, so think of me. Go, comfort
your cousin; I must say she is dead; and so,
farewell.

Borachio and Conrade were being questioned by Dogberry, Verges, and the Sexton[1]. Dogberry was very talkative and bossy. He loved ordering people around. He commanded the Sexton to write everything down.

Gradually they pieced together the details of the evil plot. The watchmen had overheard Borachio boasting that he had caused the Lady Hero to be falsely accused. The Sexton said that, as a result of Borachio's treachery, Claudio had indeed accused Hero of being unfaithful, causing her to die of grief and shock. Don John had secretly left the town that morning.

Leonato must be told the truth at once. The Sexton hurried away to prepare him. Dogberry, feeling very important indeed, prepared to lead the watchmen and the two prisoners to Leonato's house.

[1]Sexton – one of the officials of the town

SEXTON: Prince John is this morning secretly stolen away;
Hero was in this manner accused, in this very
manner refused, and upon the grief of this
suddenly died.

ACT 5

Meanwhile, Leonato and Antonio happened to meet Don Pedro and Claudio. Leonato accused Claudio of causing his daughter's death. He and Antonio challenged Claudio to a fight. They shouted and exchanged angry words. Don Pedro refused to listen to them any longer. Frustrated, Antonio and Leonato went on their way.

Claudio and Don Pedro continued on their way and came across Benedick. They were pleased to see him, thinking he would cheer them up with his witty conversation. They were mistaken. He too called Claudio a villain and challenged him to a fight.

Don Pedro and Claudio did not take this seriously and tried to tease Benedick about Beatrice, but Benedick had turned against his former friends. He told Don Pedro that he would not associate with him any more, and warned Claudio again about the duel. Angrily, he told Don Pedro that his brother Don John had run away from Messina.

BENEDICK: You are a villain; I jest not. I will make it good how you dare, with what you dare, and when you dare. Do me right, or I will protest your cowardice. You have killed a sweet lady, and her death shall fall heavy on you. Let me hear from you.

Much Ado About Nothing

On the way to Leonato's house, the watchmen and
their prisoners met Don Pedro and Claudio. Dogberry
started to tell his story, but Don Pedro became
impatient with his wordiness[1]. Borachio, by now very
ashamed of what he had done, confessed everything:
how Don John wanted to cause trouble for Claudio
and Hero, how he, Borachio, had persuaded Margaret
to dress in Hero's clothes, and how they had acted
out the scene at Hero's window knowing that Don
Pedro and Claudio were watching.

Now, Hero was dead and Borachio knew it was all
his fault. He deserved, he said, to be punished.
Claudio heard the conversation with horror, suddenly
remembering how much he loved Hero. He wished
himself dead.

It was obvious to Don Pedro that his brother, Don
John, was behind the plot and, to save himself, he
had escaped from Messina.

[1]wordiness – Dogberry used big words but in the wrong way,
and his speeches were confusing.

DON PEDRO: Runs not this speech like iron through your blood?

CLAUDIO: I have drunk poison whiles he uttered it.

DON PEDRO: But did my brother set thee on to this?

BORACHIO: Yes, and paid me richly for the practice of it.

In the meantime, the Sexton had told Leonato and Antonio about Borachio's confession. Leonato, however, wanted Claudio to suffer a little longer.

He met with Claudio and told him to put a tribute to Hero on her tomb, and come to his house the next morning. His brother Antonio had a daughter, he said, who was just like Hero. If Claudio married Antonio's daughter, all would be forgiven. Claudio agreed immediately.

Leonato thought that Margaret should be punished also for her part in the plot but Borachio assured him that Margaret was innocent. She hadn't realised that this was a plot against her friend.

Dogberry was angry because Borachio had called him an ass during the questioning. That should be taken into account, he said. Leonato, wanting to shut him up, thanked Dogberry for his trouble and gave him a reward. Dogberry was very happy.

LEONATO: My brother hath a daughter,
          Almost the copy of my child that's dead,
          And she alone is heir to both of us.
          Give her the right you should have given her
          cousin,
          And so dies my revenge.

Benedick couldn't stop thinking about Beatrice. He begged Margaret to send her to him in the garden. As he waited, he tried to compose a love song. This was something new for him and very difficult. He couldn't make the words rhyme, and decided he was not a poet after all.

At last Beatrice came and wanted to know what had happened between Benedick and Claudio. Benedick told her that he had challenged Claudio to a duel. If Claudio did not respond soon, he would be called a coward.

Then, becoming tender, he asked Beatrice what had caused her to fall in love with him. Beatrice answered in a gentle, teasing way. Benedick didn't mind. They were too old, he said, to behave as young lovers did.

Ursula interrupted them with the latest news: there was great excitement at Leonato's house. Lady Hero had been proved innocent, Don Pedro and Claudio now realised they had been deceived, and Don John, the cause of all the trouble, had escaped.

URSULA: Madam, you must come to your uncle. Yonder's old coil at home; it is proved my Lady Hero hath been falsely accused, the Prince and Claudio mightily abused, and Don John is the author of all, who is fled and gone. Will you come presently?

Later that night, Claudio, Don Pedro and Balthasar the musician, visited the family tomb as Leonato had ordered. Claudio read a poem in praise of the dead Hero, and swore that he would do this every year on the anniversary of her death.

Balthasar sang a special song.

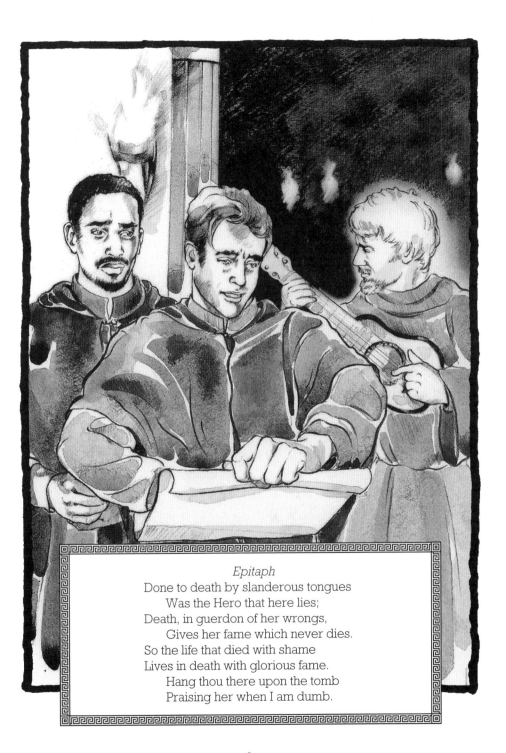

Epitaph
Done to death by slanderous tongues
    Was the Hero that here lies;
Death, in guerdon of her wrongs,
    Gives her fame which never dies.
So the life that died with shame
Lives in death with glorious fame.
    Hang thou there upon the tomb
    Praising her when I am dumb.

Leonato's family and the Friar were gathered at
Leonato's house. The Friar was very happy. He had
known from the beginning that Hero was innocent.
They all agreed that the Prince and Claudio had done
no wrong, having been deceived by Don John.

Now Leonato would have his little revenge on
Claudio. He told Beatrice, Hero, and her ladies to
leave the room and return, wearing veils, when he
sent for them. Antonio was to pretend that Hero was
his daughter and 'give' her to Claudio.

Benedick took the opportunity to tell Leonato that he
and Beatrice were in love and asked Leonato's
permission to marry her. Leonato immediately
agreed. The Friar said that he would be very happy
to perform the ceremony.

BENEDICK: Friar, I must entreat your pains, I think.
FRIAR: To do what, signor?
BENEDICK: To bind me, or undo me – one of them.
Signor Leonato, truth it is, good signor,
Your niece regards me with an eye of favour.

Don Pedro and Claudio arrived as planned. Claudio was prepared to marry Antonio's daughter, as he had agreed.

The ladies returned, wearing veils, and Antonio gave 'his daughter' to Claudio. Claudio took her hand and asked her to marry him.

When Hero threw back her veil, Claudio was amazed and delighted. How could it be? Another Hero? Don Pedro exclaimed that this must be the real Hero come back from the dead.

Leonato said that, in fact, this was his daughter Hero. She had been dead, he explained, so long as people believed the terrible lie about her.

The Friar promised to explain everything properly after they had made their marriage vows.

DON PEDRO: The former Hero! Hero that is dead!
LEONATO: She died, my lord, but whiles her slander lived.

Now that Claudio and Hero were happy, there was time at last for Benedick and Beatrice. But when Benedick asked Beatrice if she loved him, she tried to pretend she wasn't in love at all.

But Claudio had found one of the love poems that Benedick had tried to write for Beatrice, while Hero had a similar one in Beatrice's handwriting, written for Benedick. They could no longer deny their love for each other. With a passionate kiss, Benedick made sure that for once Beatrice couldn't talk back.

To complete the happiness of the day, a messenger brought the news that Don John had been captured and was being brought back to Messina. Don John could wait until tomorrow, said Benedick. He would enjoy thinking up a suitable punishment for him.

The pipers played, and they all danced.

CLAUDIO: And I'll be sworn upon't that he loves her,
For here's a paper written in his hand,
A halting sonnet of his own pure brain,
Fashioned to Beatrice.

HERO: And here's another
Writ in my cousin's hand, stolen from her pocket,
Containing her affection unto Bendick.